wilted
lilies

wilted lilies

WILTED LILY Series
— Book One —

Kelli Owen

Gypsy Press

Dedication: For Raynebow, the tiniest
and strongest of us all.

Acknowledgements — Jacob Haddon, for
excitedly saying "yes, that one!" after hearing the
opening pages (causing this to originally appear
as a 4-part serial in his quarterly magazine
Lamplight). Bob Ford for helping me sprinkle
Southern lingo into my Northern Midwestern
girl's prose. Bob Ford, Tod Clark, Dave Thomas
and Ron Dickie for their exuberant use of red
pens and wagging fingers. And this time, Lily
May, for coming to life and speaking to me like
no other character... don't worry, honey, we're
not done.

People need hard times and oppression
to develop psychic muscles.

— Emily Dickinson

wilted lilies

"Meemaw said I was an old soul. Mamma always said I had the shine. Papa…" The light-eyed girl picked at something invisible on her skirt. "Papa was afraid of me.

"You see, I knew things. I don't know how. I just did. Mamma says I been like that since I was little. Oh I didn't know nothing useful. Didn't know the lotto numbers or how many gumballs were in the jar at the fair. But I knew when people was gonna pass." She leaned closer and whispered, "And I could hear things."

She licked her lips and stared at the pattern in her skirt. The man could see she was remembering rather than talking. He had learned long ago, silence would get people to open up much easier than asking. He waited.

"If I let my insides get real, real quiet, I could hear what people were thinking… It's like they was thinking too loud when they was in turmoil or hurtin'. I didn't mean to. And I didn't want to. But I couldn't turn it off. Fact is, when I was little I thought everyone could do it. I thought it was normal.

"It wasn't anything close to normal. And Sussex County is the last place you wanna be different. It's too small. Too tight. I don't have no friends—not 'cos the kids don't like me, but 'cos their folks don't want 'em near me. My family was shunned because of me. Mamma and Papa and Meemaw with me. But they were okay with that, mostly."

Her fingers went up to a closed locket hanging on a tarnished chain around her neck.

"I suppose you want to know about that Jenkins boy, though."

He nodded, leaning closer to the tape recorder between them.

"It started in church." She sat back and closed her eyes, smiling as if she could see something beautiful and peaceful behind those lids.

"I was singing the praises of the Lord at the top of my lungs. I wasn't singing in church, you see, I was singing beyond the church, towards heaven, so's He could hear my voice above the rest. It was a warm spring day, and I was wearing a new dress. It was perfect. And then I heard it.

"In the middle of the second hallelujah, clear as if it was whispered right into my ear, someone said 'I'm going to kill her.' I stopped singing. I looked around, wondering who could think such a thing during church—and during praise. I felt real funny. Like my insides were twisting in on themselves and my heart was pounding too hard but too slow. That was the last inside voice I heard from the living."

The girl opened her eyes, wet with glassy tears. She wasn't necessarily crying, but brimming with emotion like some do at a wedding, or when remembering someone who's been gone for too long. She caught his gaze and held him there, trapped, even though her focus was past him into something only she could see.

Her body frame and posture were true to her young age, but those silver eyes held years far beyond her own. It was like staring at the moon, and he couldn't decide if they were an extremely light blue or truly silver in nature. Her bottom lip quivered, and she broke the unintentional stare.

"World went quiet that day. Too quiet... It had been noisy for so very long. So noisy, I took to wandering the woods behind our house when I was just little, to be alone, to find quiet. I spent all my fifteen years on this earth tryin' ta' hide from everyone's insides tryin' to get out. To get away from their thoughts and fears and anger. You see, I didn't always get the happy thoughts. I rarely got to hear about love. But longing? Oh, I knew about longing. I knew who missed who, who wanted who, and it weren't always the right people. Longing is strong when folk think too loud. But fear and anger? They were always so much louder. Longing is like a whisper tickling me. Anger? Fear? Those dragged me out of whatever else I was doing and came on like unannounced dinner guests. Shucks, I used to answer my papa all the time before I realized he was thinking those thoughts and not actually sayin' 'em out loud."

She shook her head, as if she were trying to stop herself from remembering something. Or sharing it.

"Loneliness can be both. Sometimes it's just a whimper. Sometimes it's like someone's yellin' "Fire!" in a crowded church. It'll get your attention, but it's hard to tell where it's coming from. I knew exactly who it was the day Mrs. Miller tried to kill herself. That was the first time I told what someone was thinking."

The girl paused, and he waited, adjusting the recorder. He couldn't tell if she was trying to remember or trying to forget, and before he could prod her to continue, she spoke.

"I was walking home from school. Head down like I do, hoping if I didn't notice nobody, then their insides wouldn't notice me. But as I passed Mrs. Miller's front stoop, I heard her clear as a spring peeper's call. Thinking how she was gonna finish hanging the clothes out on the line, tidy up a bit, and then go down into the root cellar and hang herself. I had heard some awful stuff but that one scared me. I tried to keep walking and pretend maybe I heard it wrong. But by the time I got home I was crying something fierce, convinced God would blame me if I didn't stop her. I tried to talk to my papa, but he shushed me away and opened another beer. I found Mamma hanging our own clothes out back and ran to her. I told her what I heard and she tried to calm me and tell me it couldn't be right, that Mrs. Miller would never do that."

The girl looked up at him, truly looked at him, as if to make sure he was paying attention.

"You see, Mrs. Miller's son died the summer before. Him and his new souped-up Charger went 'round the bend by the quarry way too fast and the only thing to stop 'em both was a big ol' pine. Then her husband up and left town with some waitress, leaving her all alone—in her woes, as Mamma calls it. She was a kind lady, always nice to me. And a good God-fearing woman, too. But everyone has their breaking point. And I 'spect she'd reached hers that day. I was afraid she would go straight to hell, taking me with her for not stopping her. 'Cos if I can't believe God made me this way on purpose, to do His work, then I'm nothing but a freak—or worse, a devil child like my papa used to think.

"I was hysterical by the time Papa put his beer down and come outside to see what my screaming was all about. He slapped me across the face. Hard. I don't know if it was to get my attention and calm me, or just because he'd been waiting for a chance to do it. But it worked. I stopped screaming. I cried and pleaded with Mamma, knowin' Papa was there but not really 'specting him to do nothing 'bout it. Shocked me when he said he'd go check on Mrs. Miller if it would shut me up."

The girl's tiny hand went to her chest, and she grimaced more than smiled.

"Papa got there right as she was climbing up on the chair, noose already dangling above her. I saved her, but I lost something that day. Papa was even meaner to me after that, like the proof I heard things drove home his feelings for me. It wasn't that he hated me, but his fear was so bad I might as well have been the devil himself. And Mrs. Miller? They took her away to the hospital for a bit, and when she got out she didn't thank me at all. Her thoughts were always cloudy around me, like she was blocking me out—but they cleared on occasion, and I knew she was upset I had stopped her and forced her to keep on living. She rectified that a couple years later by swallowing all them pills she got from those doctors. I still wonder why God wanted me to save her. Maybe she did something in them two years that changed someone else. I don't know. I just don't.

"But that was the first time I told anyone

what I heard. Oh everyone knew I could hear 'em. But now I had gone and shared a secret. Shared their inner whispers. It didn't matter I did it to save someone. And that was when everyone really started looking at me funny and keeping their young'uns away. That was when everything changed the first time. But in the church, when it went all quiet, that was different. I was glad for the quiet, but it also scared me. It was strange to me, like being deaf all of a sudden. And worse, I had heard someone threaten someone else and didn't know who it was. I was panicked. I was about to be a murderer, 'cos knowing and not doing anythin' 'bout it was just as good as doin' it myself.

She grabbed her skirt in her fingers and pinched at the material as she twisted it. She swallowed audibly.

"Do you want a glass of water, hon?" He raised an eyebrow and waited to see if she remembered he was sitting there.

She shook her head. "No, I just want to be done with it."

"Okay. Can you tell me when you started hearing the other voices?"

She nodded, swallowed hard again, and sighed.

"Weren't long after that day in church when I started hearing other things. See, after Sunday services we all gather in the church basement for a big lunch. Then the kids go out and play in the front yard. I usually end up walking through the graves out back to find quiet. At least, I used to. The quiet had been so loud after a couple days, it was almost normal at that point. I was almost used to it. But at the back of the graves, where the daisies start tangling with the honeysuckle and brambles, it was anything but quiet. I could hear things again all of a sudden, like when your ears pop and everything seems really loud. I looked around the cemetery to try and find who I was hearing."

Her eyes got wider as she spoke, and she stopped abruptly, snapping her head up at him.

"But I suppose I have ta' tell you 'bout the Jenkins boy first, so's you understand what came after."

He nodded and glanced at the clock on the wall before eyeballing the recorder between them.

"After the county fair packed up and left town the summer before that day in church, the cleanup crew found little Tommy Jenkins dead. It was a heck of a shock to everyone. But it wasn't just that he was dead, laying facedown among the trash and weeds in the trampled field. It was that this was the second time he was found dead."

"The second time?" He furrowed his brow and watched, as the dam behind her brimming eyes broke.

A flood of tears flowed down the girl's face, she sniffled, then quivered her lips at him before managing to speak. "May I use the facilities?"

The simple sentence took more than he'd expected, both in the amount of time to get the words out and in the apparent strength to say out loud. He nodded. Almost immediately the steel door opened and a female officer entered, and the girl questioned him with one raised eyebrow.

"Come with me, honey." The female officer led the girl from the room and left him alone with his thoughts. He pushed STOP on the recorder.

Officer Travis Butler pushed back the uncomfortable chair with a squeak of resistance on the worn tile floor and stood. He stretched his arms above his head and bent at the hip in both directions to relieve the tension in his back. He turned to the mirror behind him, blinked several times, and shook his head. A quiet tapping on the glass let him know his presence was requested, and he left the small interrogation room only to enter the door immediately to his left.

The room was mostly dark, a small desk lamp illuminating the doorway and him as he stepped inside. In the corner a figure sat, only the clean pleated black slacks and shiny cowboy boots poking from the bottom was visible in the dimness of the room. He had no upper body, no face, and would have unnerved anyone unaware of his presence. But Travis knew he was there—knew he was watching.

"Do you really expect me to believe all this?" he questioned the shadows.

"You don't have to believe anything, Officer. You let her talk. Let her ramble through her story any way she needs to. When she's done, we'll see if there are any answers or clarifications we need. And then we decide what to believe. Not you. It's not your job."

"Then why am I here?" He cocked his head, irritated to be called to a neighboring county on his day off for no apparent reason.

"Because you don't know her. You don't know this town. You're not tainted with any of the history that may or may not come out of her young mouth or tender memory. We need you because you're…" the shadow paused, looking for the right word. "Innocent."

Travis rolled his eyes, more for his own exasperation than for the man in the shadows to see, and turned toward the one-way mirror in time to see the female officer escort the girl back to her chair.

He closed the door without another word, leaving the man in the darkness to watch, and nodded to the female office as they passed in the doorway of the interrogation room.

"Better?" He addressed the girl as he reached

to push RECORD on the tape player before even sitting down.

She nodded without looking up. "Thank you."

"Okay, then, Miss Holloway—"

"Lily May."

"Lillian," he acquiesced. "About the Jenkins boy then?"

"Lily, please." The pleading in her eyes reminded him of a wounded animal. "Lily May is what they call me. Only person ever called me Lillian was that man."

He nodded, not wanting to press the point of the man yet. "Okay then, Lily, what about Tommy Jenkins?"

"Tommy drowned three years back, when he was only little—four years old at the time. He was playing down by the little run-off crick that runs through the fields behind the Rows him and his folk live in. You know, down there on Willow Road, where all them houses look the same? The rains were bad that month and made the waters higher than their normal trickle. He didn't know, couldn't remember, if he fell or slipped, but he ended up facedown in the waters unconscious and drowned there. His mamma found him and the neighbor came running when he heard her screaming. He did that CPR thing on him, and they brought him back.

"I didn't know Tommy or his family when this happened. Didn't know nobody in the Rows there. But my meemaw was in the hospital—she was recovering from what they said was a heart attack, but she disagreed, causing a heck of a stink with the doctors—and I was there visiting when they came in with him. It was such a commotion, so many voices—spoken and not—I couldn't stomach the fear and pain, and I shut Meemaw's door."

She pulled at the dried mud on her dress, absently plucking it free from the material and dropping it on the floor before habitually smoothing out the fabric across her knees.

"Meemaw finished telling me how to pull and clean the garden huckleberries for pie—gotta be the white flowered berries, the shiny ones from the black nightshade, she said. Never the green ones, or the red ones from the purple flowered patches. Those are poisonous, you know, and awful dangerous to even touch. So I had to shut the door and listen close as she told me. I didn't know what was going on in the hall after that. I didn't know Tommy had been brought in with an ambulance or that his family and neighbors were all beside themselves stumbling over each other to get to his side.

"When I left Meemaw's room a bit later it was calm in the long hallways again. I made for the door, head down—hospitals are horrible places for normal people, but they just hurt me to be near them, let alone inside. So much noise.

So much pain and worry. I couldn't walk fast enough down that hallway. I was thinking of the berries and the pie my papa loved so much, and trying to fill my head with my own thoughts so those around me couldn't get it. As I was about to turn and take the side exit out by where the nurses all gather, a little voice come out of the room at the end of the hall and said, 'I love huckleberries.'

"I froze and turned around in a circle, trying to figure out where it had come from. I almost didn't see his tiny little body under those covers in that big ol' bed. But there was Tommy Jenkins, smiling at me all happy. Like he hadn't just died. I told him I didn't say anything about any berries, and he argued with me. We went back and forth a couple minutes before we both stopped. I imagine my eyes must'a been about as wide as his, when I realized I hadn't actually spoken out loud during any of our argument— but neither had he. I slipped into his room and shut the door behind me."

Lily fingered the locket again and looked up at Travis.

"You can't imagine what it was like after so long. Someone could hear my thoughts...like I always did to other people. After years and years of the noisiest silent treatment you can imagine, I wasn't alone no more."

She sniffled back tears and blinked. "I really

miss Tommy."

Travis put an elbow on the table and leaned his chin against his fist. "So Tommy could hear people like you claim you can?" He corrected himself, "Could."

"Just like me. We didn't know how much or how well until after he got out of the hospital, and we had some time to work through it, but yes, just like me. It scared him 'cos he could hear the doctors thoughts and his mamma's fears. But he recovered quick and was released in a couple days. He snuck out of the Rows and down to the woods behind my house to meet me.

"He said he told his mamma, but she shushed him and told him to never say anything like that again. He kept trying to talk to her and his papa, but they just put him in his room or told him to go play. I 'spect they were afraid of him like everyone had always been of me. People don't want you knowing everything they think. It wipes away the lies they tell themselves and let's you see the monsters hiding inside. The monsters they pretend don't exist."

Lily looked at Travis without blinking for several moments, intensely studying his eyes as if to find his monster. He shifted uncomfortably and reached for his glass of water, breaking eye contact.

"After a couple weeks, his mamma showed up at our house after dinner one night and asked to talk to my mamma. Mamma made iced tea for them, and they went out back, away from the rest of us to talk. When Tommy's mamma left, she must've walked all the way around the house to avoid me, 'cos she was gone without a word, and Mamma called me outside.

"That was when I started watching little Tommy. They called it sitting, but it was really 'spose to be more like training. They didn't want no one knowing he was a freak like me and thought I would help them keep their secret. I didn't mind. I liked playing with Tommy. He was younger than me by a big bit, but we had fun. We played games, explored the woods, and practiced on each other—both hearing each other and blocking each other, 'cos blocking was more important than listening. The only people that knew about Tommy were his family and mine, and we kept it that way. I saw his mamma give my papa money once and wondered if it was for the sitting or the silence."

"So no one else ever knew about Tommy?" Travis grabbed the pen resting on the pad of paper in front of him, finally intrigued enough to take notes.

"Not from me. Not from Tommy. And I'm pretty sure none of our families shared for shame of the secret."

"And this was how long before he was found dead?"

"'Bout two years. It was three years ago this fall when he drowned, and he was killed last summer."

"And you were babysitting him the entire time?"

"Every day after school, until dinner. And all day during the summer, until last summer when I started helping Miss Betty at the diner for extra cash for the family. I was at work when Tommy was murdered." She looked down, guilt washing across her face.

"You keep saying murdered. He was found dead, but no one was ever charged with homicide."

"He was murdered." She glared at him, unwavering in her conviction of what happened.

He wasn't going to argue with her about a different case, he needed her to get through this to the current case. "And you were at work?"

"Yeah. I was washing dishes after everyone lunched and gone. I hadn't seen him since that morning. He was scared bad though. Had been for a while. A couple weeks, maybe? Real scared. He tried to tell me he wasn't, but I could hear him. It was all jumbled and mixed up and didn't make a lick of sense to me other than I knew he was afraid. And I could see it on him, like his colors were...all muddy."

Lily swallowed and whispered, "Remember, I know when people is gonna pass. I knew. I just knew. And I couldn't do nothin' about it. I told him to stay inside, not to go anywhere or do anything without me. But the fair was in town and it was the last day, and he just had to go play on the midway one last time. Maybe if his ma and pa weren't so afraid of him, they would have gone with, but they didn't. They let him go on his own. Six years old and they just let him go. When he didn't come back for dinner, they called my mamma. We'd only just realized he was missing when the crews found him."

Lily unclenched her fist and retrieved a Kleenex to preemptively wipe her nose. Travis hadn't even realized she'd had a tight-squeeze hand or anything in it, but figured she'd gotten it when she went to the restroom and looked around for a trash can and more tissue. The tears rolled down her face, but she talked through them, the pitch of her voice rising and falling with her focus.

"You know he thought about running away near the end? He wasn't afraid of monsters under his bed, not Tommy. Tommy was brave and smart, so much smarter than me. He was afraid of a person. Someone had scared him. Scared him bad enough for him to pack his little backpack and think about living in the woods, sneaking food from me or garbage or wherever. He was just little! He weren't big enough to handle what God gave him, let alone some man scaring him. And I couldn't save him."

She clenched her jaw, her face reddening with anger and pain as she clamped her emotions inside and stared off into a place Travis couldn't see. A place he didn't think he'd like even if he could see it. Her eyes flitted back and forth, as if watching something happening, and she needed to absorb all the details. Then her expression changed, her eyes swam out of focus, and the jittering was nothing but a desperate attempt to hold on to her own calm.

"Lily?" He put a hand on the table in front of her, offering her comfort without touching. "Lily May?"

She snapped her eyes up at him, seething rage slipping away as recognition softly dissolved into being.

"Sorry."

"It's okay." He pulled his hand back. "Do you need more tissues?"

She shook her head and closed her fist around the spent Kleenex.

"Sussex County is a quiet place. We take care of our own here—our own kin, our own problems. Murders just don't happen. So Tommy being found dead with a broke neck—murdered, okay, because you don't break your neck falling in a field—it was a big deal." Her voice raised in conviction.

Travis nodded, sitting back as he

subconsciously pulled away from her anger.

"They blamed the carnies, of course. At first. 'Cos it couldn't be one of the townsfolk that killed Tommy. Couldn't be kin. The carnie workers weren't local, and even Sussex's own white trash look at them as dirty, so it made sense to put the blame on outsiders. But it didn't make sense to the law. Nothing pointed at them, no evidence of anything. Nothing was ever found, no one was ever blamed, but it didn't go away neither.

"Everyone started looking at me funny. I don't know if it got out that Tommy was different, or that I'd been babysitting him. Thing was, they only looked at me funny when they didn't think I could see them. No one made eye contact. Not for a long time after. No one would talk directly to me. Even Miss Betty. She let me go the week after they found Tommy, saying she couldn't have that around her. Whatever the heck that was."

Lily grunted a noise of frustration and looked at the mirror behind Travis, squinting as if she was trying to see through it.

"At first folk thought I was somehow to blame. Then that changed, and they were accusing me of knowing and not telling. Mamma got attacked at the market by Mr. Tipper, yelling at her right there in the cereal aisle about how the police should ask her little freak 'cos I probably knew exactly who'd done it and why and how, and if

I was protecting the killer, and Mamma was protecting me, then we should all be strung up to rot." She took a deep breath before continuing on her tirade. "But the whole time they were blaming me and thinking I knew who it was. They was avoiding me 'cos they didn't want me digging around their heads. I had only ever told three times when people was thinking something bad, and only to save their lives. Mrs. Miller from hanging herself. My math teacher, Mr. Williams, when he was worried about the pains in his chest that turned out to be a real heart attack they saved him from. And when Trudy was thinking about cutting her arms so she could 'feel the burn.' I didn't know what that meant, but it scared me. Worried me. And I told. But I saved all those people. No matter, people were afraid if I talked then, I would talk now, and that I would tell anything I learned just to get myself out of hot water. 'Cept I was never in no hot water. I never did nothin' and the police never accused me of nothin'. But it was bad. It got real weird around here for a while, even stranger than usual.

"You know, Preacher Jacob even stopped by after dinner one Saturday and asked us not to come to church? More specifically, for me not to come into the House of the Lord. And he worded it like that, like God himself had kicked me out!

"This whole time I'd done nothing but answer

questions when the police asked what we did when I was babysitting, or where we spent our time, or if I knew anything that would be helpful. I told them he was scared of someone, but I didn't know who. And when the police weren't questioning me, I was telling Tommy's mamma over and over and over, I didn't know nothing. But she kept asking, every time she saw me, like I was lying for some reason. Why would I lie? I loved Tommy like a little brother. I wanted to protect him when he was alive. I wanted to catch his murderer as much as anyone. When I wasn't answerin' questions, alls I ever did was sit at Tommy's grave, rocking back and forth crying. I was so mad at God. He gave me a friend, someone like me, and then took him away. But no one felt sorry for me. No one understood my loss. Least of all not Tommy's mamma."

Lily's hand went up to her throat, but rather than grabbing at the locket she stroked her neck as if working out a sore muscle. Her eyes glazed over, and her face went slack for a moment. The grime on her fingers seemed to stand out more against the pale creamy skin of her neck, and Travis noticed not only the dirt under her fingernails, but the raw, ragged edges of the nails, the scuffs on her knuckles, and the dried blood still caked in the creases of her joints even after washing her hands.

"I didn't see Tommy's mamma around the

side of our house when I got home from school that day. I was thinking about the other kids, the fear and anger I could hear clear as day. They pretended like nothing was wrong, but they seethed inside whenever I walked past or sat too close. I was worried Mrs. Applebee wouldn't let me help her after classes like she had the year before. I was scared the principal would kick me out just like God had. I wasn't paying attention to the world around me. I was so lost in my own thoughts, I didn't even hear his mamma shouting at me from behind her closed lips. I heard nothing."

She continued to caress her neck.

"You know how they say the edges of your sight gets blurry and everything fades to black? They're wrong. The blur is in front of you, dead center, and fast, like a flash of lightning that echoes the pain you feel. The edges aren't blurry, they're dark, but still clear enough to see motion. Clear enough to see who's choking you."

Officer Travis Butler watched the girl's face, trying to decide if her demeanor of damaged innocence was merely a mask to echo the story she was spinning. There was something about her. A quality he couldn't pinpoint, which was almost soft and seemed to calm him, something about her vibe pulled him in and held him like a hug. He found himself wanting to believe her, but logic and reason kept his blind acceptance at bay. Barely.

"I was just fixin' to give up and die. My lungs didn't hurt as much. I was suddenly just tired. But then I saw a blur of motion to the side of me. I hit the ground real sudden like. I coughed, a lot, and it hurt again, and when I opened my eyes to look around, Tommy's mamma was lying there next to me. I guess the blur had been Papa's arm, but I never asked. Not then, not since. Now, I don't know if I passed out or not. No idea how long I was lying there. But I was awake enough when Mrs. Jenkins sat up, all full of piss 'n' vinegar, like Meemaw calls it."

Lily's eyes widened as she spoke, her hand still at her throat in memory of the choking.

"She barked at my papa, screaming at the top of her lungs and waving her arms around like a crazy person. She called him names, swearing somethin' fierce and sayin' she was gonna tell the sheriff. But he just yelled right back at her. Swore all kinds of bad words and raised his fist a couple times, making her back up farther and farther to avoid being too close in case he decided to swing. I don't remember exactly what was said, but by the time he was done, his face was bright red and his anger poured right out of his eyes. You know that saying? If looks could kill? She would be deader than a spider in Mamma's kitchen. I do remember him telling her she hit a minor, 'cos it hurt me to hear I was just a minor, any ol' minor. But then he told her to never come on our property again and to never come nowhere near his daughter. I felt better then, like it was specific to me. Papa brought me down to the church where Meemaw and Mamma were for some afternoon knitting thing, and told them what happened. They took me to the hospital to make sure I was okay. Papa didn't go with us. I imagine he went home and got a beer, his part done. It was all pretty awful."

"Were charges ever pressed?"

"Oh heck no. She was pretty scared by the time she left. She was never gonna say nothin' to no one."

"No, I meant against her."

"Oh…"

Officer Travis Butler smiled at her, saddened by her assumption her father had been in the wrong for protecting her.

"No." Her brows slanted down as one corner of her mouth went up, a strange expression of thought, resembling an old man more than a young girl. "But I know she kept her distance. I ain't seen her other than in church, and even then she avoids me. Though I know she wants me dead."

"Dead? That's kind of harsh. Why would you say that?"

"Wade told me." She blinked at him, as if waiting for him to understand. Her mouth relaxed into a round hollow of understanding. "Wade Dixon, the old railroad worker who died last Thanksgiving. He told me."

"Before or after he died?" Travis wasn't sure if he was merely giving her tale the benefit of the doubt or if he really was starting to believe her.

"After."

"You want to tell me about it?"

Lily shrugged and looked at his glass. "I suppose. Can I still get a glass of water?"

"Yeah, sure thing." Travis looked behind him at the mirror and raised his eyebrows. He knew he could continue and someone would be ordered to bring the water to them. "It is awfully dry in here."

"I'm sorry. I am. I know I said no earlier, but the more I talk, the more my tongue dries out. Lately, I'm not so used to talking to the living with actual words as I am the dead with just thoughts, ya know?"

"It's okay. No apologies." He smiled, his lips thin and forced. "Now then, Wade, you said?"

"Well, see, after Tommy's mamma choked me, things kinda calmed down again. Mostly. I even got to go back to church, though Preacher Jacob never actually apologized or anything."

The door opened quietly, the female officer from earlier slipping in with an empty glass and a pitcher of water. She put it on the table, nodded at Travis, and left without a word. He poured the water into the glass for Lily and pushed it across to her. She drank half the glass without pausing and put it down in front of her, staring at the water as she spoke.

"I knew she was still mad at me. Still somehow blaming me for Tommy's death. She was talking about it to people who weren't avoiding me. So even though I couldn't hear her, I could hear them. And they had a million questions about me running through their heads if I did nothing but walk past after school or on my way to the store. If I actually stopped near them, like when Mamma was talking to someone at church and I was with her, standing all quiet and waiting, then there'd be all kinds o' things. Church was bad. I could hear so much anger and fear, hatred and sadness. It was awful, just awful. And everywhere. Even the minister wondered what I could have done to save Tommy, but he faked a smile at me and gave me communion, thinking about how the Lord would forgive me, so he didn't have to."

Lily paused, finished the water in the glass in one swallow and held it out for Travis to refill.

"But how'd Wade get involved?"

"Oh he wasn't involved. See, that day in church when it all went quiet? Part of the relief was 'cos I couldn't hear no one's thoughts no more about Mrs. Jenkins' lies. I couldn't hear her words through their heads. I couldn't hear the pain and hurt and anger. It was wonderful in a weird way. Weird, ya know, 'cos I wasn't used to it. Wasn't used to the quiet being so loud. And just when I thought I might get used to it and feel almost normal, I heard that voice in the back of the graveyard.

"Now when that happened, when I looked around, the only other person out there was a tall willowy kinda woman near a fresh grave. I knew it was fresh, the flowers were still laying on the fresh-turned dirt. Wilted, but still there. I smiled, kinda sad and nervous but wanting to be polite, toward her and her eyes flew open wide. She turned at me very suddenly, her dress swishing like she'd been dancing, and she asked 'You can see me?'"

Lily looked up at Travis. Her pale eyes swam with emotion, seeming to jump out at him in contrast to the mud-smeared face and perfectly blushed lips of youth.

"You ever thought about that? About your dead loved ones hanging around wishing you could see them? Wishing they could talk to you or hug you or whatever, one last time? I guess the shock of being seen was too much. When I nodded she put a hand to her mouth and kinda faded to nothin'. Just gone. I remember sitting down right there in the grass trying to figure out what was going on. I remember 'cos the grass was real wet and my dress got muddy. Mamma had a heck of a fit about it later. But I didn't pay no mind to my dress at the time, I just sat down and stared at the grave she had been at for some time. I'm not even sure how long I was there. When I finally got up, I figured I would stop and look, since I couldn't really get back to the church without going past it anyway. Clara Beth McDermott, it said. I'll never forget the name. Sounded like a movie star or something to me. And she was real real pretty. She coulda been a movie star, ya know? I asked Mamma about her, and she frowned. Said she was cousin to Meemaw's neighbor or something, and how she'd died giving birth to her first baby. The baby lived. She didn't. It was enough to make me cry for days. Mamma never asked why I was wondering about a random grave in the church yard, and I never told her it was when the dead talks started, right there with Clara Beth McDermott, whose dress was the same color as the dying flowers on her grave—a nice crisp white, now kinda dirty and pale at the edges."

"And Sarah led you to Wade?" Travis's impatience was starting to show, and a sharp tap on the mirror behind him reminded him to shut up and let the girl talk.

"No, sir. But I'm getting there." She smiled and looked over his shoulder at the mirror. She studied it a minute and then turned her attention back to him.

"The following Sunday, Clara Beth was back at her grave. This time she was waiting for me to see her as much as I was wondering if I would. 'You're the girl that can hear people's thoughts, aren't you?' she asked me. I nodded. She held her hand out, offering it to me to shake, I suppose, but pulled back immediately when she realized I couldn't touch her anymore than normal people could see her. 'I'm Clara Beth,' she said, as she turned her head and looked down at her own gravestone."

Lily's eyes glazed over—her focus once again not on Travis, but rather on the memory. He let her drift for a moment, while she revisited that day in the graveyard.

"Clara Beth was so kind. Well, when I met her anyway. That first time we talked helped us both so much, I think. We were sorta lost in the world of the dead, it being new to both of us. I told her my name and how I was sorry she died. Clara Beth didn't remember dying. Not at all. She said she remembered being in pain with the baby coming and all, but then she just got real, real tired. Next thing she knew, she was standing at her own grave—alone, scared, and awful confused about everything. I was upset when she told me about dying. I mean, no heaven? I spent my whole life praising God, praying and singing to Him, and here was a girl telling me there was no heaven?"

Lily exhaled in a huff, frustrated. Travis watched her, understanding completely as she reeled at the fact the afterlife wasn't necessarily what she'd been taught.

"Clara Beth asked me a whole bunch of questions, real quick like, but I don't know if she really wanted answers so much as to just scream the questions to a God she suddenly wasn't sure about. I did the only thing I could… I asked questions back. I asked if she was a good person and she swore she was—sayin' she'd always done what her parents and God told her. She said she was a good wife and would have been a good mother, but that last part made her cry when she said it. I think maybe it was the first time she realized she wasn't there anymore to be a mother. She cried, you know, and I could see it—plain as if I could wipe her tears away."

Lily paused and stared at her lap. An almost inaudible sigh, followed by a slow blink, and Lily inhaled as she looked up at Travis.

"I'm sorry. Clara Beth was so nice. That first time we talked was just so hard. It's hard to think about."

"It's okay, hon. Continue when you're ready."

"If we wait for that, we'll be here 'til Christmas. Mamma says there are some things you're just never good with, even if you get used to 'em, but you just gotta do 'em anyway. I think this might be one o' them things." She cleared her throat. "I asked Clara Beth a bunch more questions. I did want the answers to 'em all, but I didn't have no idea what order to put them in, so they kinda all spilled out together. She said she had been there since the day before the first time I saw her. Said she was all alone in the graveyard, just her and her flowers. She smiled a little at that, I remember that part real well, 'cos she thought her husband Derek had remembered her favorite flowers were lilies. Even though they were wilted, they were still there for her and that made her happy. I nodded at her and told her Mamma had named me so, because the flowers were used for Easter and weddin's. I didn't tell her Papa was always sure to point out they were more common for funerals. Clara Beth tried to touch 'em, but her hand went through the stems like smoke through a screen door. It's still strange to me when the dead move through things like that, they look so real to me.

"I asked Clara Beth if she could leave. She said she could, and she had. She spent time in her house watching her husband and new baby boy. But she couldn't touch them, couldn't quiet the little one's fussing, and that hurt her something fierce. So she left and went back to the graveyard. That was when I first saw her. Why she was so sad and so shocked when I saw her."

Lily plucked mud from her dress and put it on the table. She looked up at Travis.

"My dress looks a little like hers did—a dirty wreck, but for different reasons."

Travis leaned forward, ready for her to start talking about The Man.

"She told me about another ghost, the only other one she'd seen. A real nice old black woman, she said. Clara Beth said she was sitting on the church steps like she was waiting for someone. The old woman never gave Clara Beth her name, but she said she was buried nearby—without a marker—and that she'd been dead for so long, she barely remembered being alive. The old woman knew a lot about a lot of things, but almost nothing about other things. She couldn't answer Clara Beth about why she was here in her dirty dinner dress. But she could tell her why that dress, and why it was dirty."

Lily May leaned in, her eyes growing wide as she nodded slightly.

"You see, the dead appear in what they know. They don't know what they're buried in, but they know their own clothing. And they usually look like they feel, so if they're upset, they might look all a fright, but if they're at peace they might look really nice and clean. But the longer the dead stay here instead of moving on, the more they can control their appearance.

Then they can change it however and whenever they wanna."

Lily May nodded again, tilting her head to the side just enough for Travis to automatically nod back at the gesture.

"And the old woman knew about the flowers." Lily returned her attention to the drying dirt on the fabric across her lap. "The old woman ghost—who I never could find, even when I went looking for her—told Clara Beth when folk died too sudden, or had things they felt were too important left undone, they would sometimes stay behind. But it took them a while to materialize. They never showed up until their funeral flowers were droopy. She told Clara Beth, she thought it was so folk couldn't see their own funeral, 'cos no one should see that, or see the ones they loved until they'd had a couple days to get past the worst of the mourning. And she said if they didn't figure it out before the flowers were completely decayed, they would be stuck here forever, like she was. I don't know how true that part is, but that's what she told Clara Beth."

"So ghosts don't appear until after the flowers are wilted? Do you hear them before they appear?" Travis took a drink of water.

Lily shook her head. "No, sir. And I don't always talk to them. They don't always want to talk to me. Sometimes they avoid me."

"I see. And did Mrs. McDermott leave when her flowers died?"

"No." Lily fidgeted in the metal chair, the soft pads of her bare feet tapping against the legs of the chair.

Travis wondered why no one had found socks or shoes, or even crime scene booties, to give the girl to cover her feet. He knew she would have been wrapped in a blanket when they found her, but even that was gone before Travis started his interview.

"I mean, she's gone, but not 'cos her flowers are. The next day I saw her and she had been at her house again. She was very upset. She remembered she'd been hiding money in a coffee can behind the loose board in the cellar. She was keeping it for emergencies but hoped it would be for a vacation with the baby instead. She had never told Derek about it. She asked me to tell him where it was.

"It took me a couple days to work up the courage. I just wasn't sure how to go about telling a complete stranger his dead wife told me a secret she'd never told him. I didn't need any more whispers about me in town. I didn't need more angry rumors or people wanting to dig around inside my head or shunning me even more because now I wasn't only hearing them, but their dead kin, too."

"Understandable." Travis nodded, again

slightly surprised at his barely contained willingness to believe her at her word.

"I finally did tell him. I don't think he believed me right away. But you know, as I was standing there on his front porch, listening to the baby fussing inside the screen and hearing Clara Beth coo to it, I saw something in his eyes change. Like a light bulb went off over his head telling him, If she could hear thoughts, why not the dead? He nodded and slipped back inside. He never offered me a seat or drink while we spoke, and he never said thank you when I left. He went back to what he was doing, like I hadn't been there. Clara Beth told me after school the next day that he did actually go down and find the tin in the cellar. She said he sat down there and cried for a long time, talking to her as if she were right there and never knowing she actually was. She kinda smiled, in a weird pinched way, like she was in pain. I never saw her after that. I don't rightly know if she went on up to heaven or not." Lily May shrugged. "Maybe she decided to stick around the house and watch her baby grow. I don't know. I saw Derek in church the next week. He smiled and gave a little nod. That was all the thanks I got, and frankly, more than I expected."

"And Wade?"

"Oh yeah. Well, see..." She took a quick drink, and looked up at Travis with clear eyes.

The pain of remembering her first meeting with Clara all but gone from her expression, she could talk like the topic was nothing more than homework. "After that I started hearing and seeing the dead when they were desperate. I don't know how they knew, maybe Clara Beth told the old woman and she spread the news, but they showed up when they wanted. I still haven't figured out if it's 'cos they can't move on or won't, but I know they don't have to be freshly dead either. I mean, the new ghosts can't do anything until their flowers are dying, but the long dead? They can pop in whenever they want. And they do. They show up in my bedroom when I'm trying to sleep, in front of my desk at school, wherever. Funny thing, some of them want to apologize. They shunned me when they were alive, but are sorry now that they're dead—maybe they think they have to apologize to get into heaven. Or worse, they need me now. Sometimes they need me to pass on information like Clara Beth did. Sometimes it's to confess 'cos I'm the only one who can hear their confession now. But sometimes, sometimes it's just to chat."

"Chat? Like visiting a living person?" Travis raised an eyebrow.

"Exactly like that. I don't know if they were afraid of moving on or just lonely, but a couple will stop by and tell me stories and share memories and meander through their thoughts for a bit to pass the time—mostly Wade and Della. Della's a nice older woman who never really believed in God, so she stayed behind, thinking there wasn't anywhere else to go. Usually, though, after they talk to me, they move on. Like maybe they just had to talk to somebody one last time. Usually. 'Cept Wade and Della, I don't think they're going anywhere.

"Wade usually tells me hunting stories or about his brothers and such, but the one day he showed up at my bedtime all a fluster. I made rules, I had to, and I told all of them they shouldn't sneak up on me or scare me or spy on me or come into my room when I'm changing or bathing. 'Cos it's just rude, you know?"

She paused and looked at him, as if waiting for him to agree. Travis realized she wasn't continuing while she stared at him and nodded. "Yes, I can see that."

"Wade knew the rules, and he came rushing in anyway. I had just crawled under the covers and was fixin' to shut out the light when he came on in and screeched to a halt at the end of my bed. I hollered at him with a harsh whisper, 'fraid to wake Papa, and told Wade he wasn't supposed to come in like that. But he told me to hush and listen 'cos it was important. Well, of course, I did.

"Seems he'd been roaming the neighborhood, walking through people's backyards and making their dogs bark. Wade's nice enough, he is, but he has a wicked streak and loves to get the pets all riled up. They can see him, too, you know. You ever seen a dog start barking at nothing? You might want to say hello, there's probably someone standing there you can't see."

Lily pursed her lips and gave a single nod to the officer, punctuating her point. He merely blinked and tried not to let her see how the thought of someone he couldn't see being in his house was unnerving to him.

"Anyway, Wade was walking through the yards harassing the dogs when he heard her and stopped. Tommy's mamma was out in her backyard sitting in the dark next to the cherry tree she had planted in his honor. She fiddled with the packed dirt, picked at the bark, and spoke to no one but the moon...and without knowing, Wade. She told Tommy she missed him and would get me back for whatever I'd done, or not done, to save her son, sayin' I would 'get my due.' Wade quoted her on that. And how she wished me dead but didn't want to go to hell for doing it herself, so she hoped and prayed God would do it for her. He didn't tell me the specifics, but I guess she went into some detail about how I could die this way or that, and what my corpse would look like, and why I should be rotting in the ground instead of her son. It was very disturbing. Wade realized he'd upset me and tried to comfort me, but he couldn't do much 'cept apologize for even telling me. Like Meemaw says, you can't unmake oatmeal, so I was stuck with the knowledge of how murderously deep her hatred for me burrowed into her soul."

She pouted for a moment and picked more mud from her dress.

"I didn't do nothin' to Tommy. I never did nothin' to nobody to deserve to die like she wants me to."

"You said they move on after you see them?" Travis tried to steer her train of thought away from Mrs. Jenkins.

"Yeah. After they tell me their stories or apologize to me, if they gotta confess, or if it's that they need me to do something for them or pass a message, then yeah, they go. Sometimes they smile first, but after whatever is keeping them here is done, they fade out, kinda like fog does in the morning. It'll be real thick, then it's not, then it's…gone. 'Cos you gotta remember, they're not see-through to me. They look just like you and me. I wouldn't know they were a ghost until I tried to touch them sometimes."

Her eyes shimmered with the threat of new tears, and her face twisted into some painful memory.

"Like Tommy. I can't touch Tommy. Lord knows I want to. I want to hug him and hold on and never let go. I was so happy to see him again. I loved him so much, like he was my own little brother."

She looked at Travis, or rather into Travis like she was looking for an answer. He shifted against her stare.

"You ever love someone so much and have them be there, right there in front of you, and alls you wanna do is grab them and hold them and never let go...but you can't? You know what that feels like? It's probably one of the worst pains I've ever felt. And it don't go away. Not ever. You just sort of...accept it."

She wiped a single tear from her eye, smudging dirt across her cheek.

"So Tommy came back?" Travis glanced behind him at the mirror.

"Oh yes. But I didn't get a chance to want to hug him the first time I saw him. The first time I saw Tommy, I didn't have a chance to do anything other than run."

She glanced at the corner of the room to her left, as if she were doing nothing more than checking the time on a wall clock.

"Tommy appeared in front of me as I was walking home from school about a month back. Just showed up right there in the middle of the sidewalk like he was walking home himself, but he looked afraid. Completely and utterly terrified. His arms were stretched out to try to stop me, and he simply said 'Turn around and go back now!' And he rushed at me. It scared me. Scared the dang daylights out of me, so I turned and ran. I got half a block when I heard the crash and turned back to look.

"Wouldn't you know it, a big ol' dump truck had gone off the road and smashed the fence I would have been standing at if I had kept going. Next to the fence, Tommy stood smiling, beaming like he just got a new puppy or something. Tommy saved me. And he knew it."

She smiled at the nothing next to her.

"That was when I learned...much as I know 'cos of hearing people's thoughts and talking to those that passed, the dead know more." Lily looked back to Travis, her eyes full of wisdom and fear. "The dead...they know lots more."

"What do you mean the dead know more? Like they have knowledge we don't have access to?" Officer Travis Butler thought of every comment—theory or belief—he'd ever heard about heaven offering answers to all life's questions.

"I don't know how much or why, but yes, they know things. I've seen Della cry 'cos she knew something was about to happen or someone was gonna die. Now see, that's not all that special to me, 'cos I know when people are gonna pass. But I don't know other things before they happen— like how Tommy knew that truck was gonna crash. And I sure can't go back and forth in time

49

like some of them say they can."

"Back and forth in time?"

Lily nodded uncomfortably, but offered no more on the subject, glancing around the room and fidgeting in her chair.

"You mind if I stand for a while? I'm awful stiff. I've been sitting for…how long you say I was gone?"

"Two weeks. And sure, you can stand. Whatever makes you comfortable." Travis pushed his chair away from the table a little and leaned back. He knew the recorder would catch anything in the room with his sensitive microphone, but wondered if her movement would cause problems with the sound. He needed to test it, and he needed to appear relaxed to keep her calm, rather than hunching over the notepad on the table while she talked. She was just a girl, and to get to the truth, to get her to open up, he'd have to make her comfortable.

"Lily May, let's get you something to eat, okay?" It was more of a directive than suggestion. "Then you can tell me more. Maybe how they move through time. Or maybe about the man."

At the mention of the man Lily flinched as if slapped, but rather than paying attention to Travis, she glanced next to her as she stood from the chair, a look of worry passed over her face. She shifted her weight from right leg to left and back again, and walked to the far end of the table.

"Okay."

"I'll be right back." Travis slipped out the door long enough to grab a uniformed office from the hallway and return.

"The officer will bring you down to the vending machine. It's not much, but it's convenient and there's a little bit of variety for you to pick from."

Lily nodded and followed the officer out of the room. The door closed softly behind them, but Travis didn't notice it. He was already in motion in the little room.

Leaning over the table he glanced to make sure RECORD was depressed on the machine, not remembering if he'd turned it off when he left the room. Seeing it on, he began his test.

"Testing sound," he spoke to the room at large. He walked around the table and tapped the corners as he passed them, moved the chair Lily had been sitting in, walked to the farthest corner of the room and turned back to the table. "Back corner should she pace that far," he kept his voice at a medium level. He returned to the table and sat down, pushing STOP on the machine as he did so.

Travis rewound the tape for a few moments and then hit PLAY. He clearly heard the door shut on the tape, followed by his own voice and tapping on the table. The chair sliding was audible but took him a moment before he understood what the sound was. "Back corner should she pace that far" came across as clear as if he'd been at the table when he said it. Satisfied, he pushed STOP and rewound, moving the tape back to where they'd left off. He pushed PLAY to test his position.

"…'cos I know when people are gonna pass."

Travis heard Lily and pressed the button marked FF to fast forward the tape a couple seconds, knowing this was near the end of their conversation.

"Back and forth in time?"

He heard his own voice and moved his finger over the FF button again.

"Don't you dare tell him!"

Travis pulled his hand back and stared at the machine, catching his breath at a voice, which was neither his nor Lily's. The tape crackled with the sound of dead air for a few moments, then Lily's voice resumed their conversation.

"Do you mind if I stand…"

Travis hit STOP, his eyes flitting without focus between the recorder and the table it sat on. He rewound the tape for a beat and hit PLAY again, leaning in closer.

"…in time?"

"Don't you dare tell him!"

Travis hit STOP and snapped to an upright position in his chair.

"What the hell…?"

His heart pounded in his chest as his hand went up to cover his mouth. The possibilities and probabilities of what he'd heard battled with his reason. He rewound the tape, hit PLAY, and held his breath as he listened.

"Back and forth in time?"

"Don't you dare tell him!"

Travis heard the other voice, again. Clear as if the speaker had been in the room. His eyes narrowed as he processed it—male, young, quite possibly…was that a child's voice? Tommy? Could it be possible? Could she be telling the truth about the dead speaking? Travis blinked as a chill ran up his spine. If not Tommy, who?

Lily's voice continued. "You mind if I stand for a while? I'm awful stiff. I've been sitting for…how long you say I was gone?"

"Two weeks. And sure, you can stand. Whatever makes you comfortable."

Travis heard what he now knew to be the sound of a chair moving against the floor, followed by his own voice.

"Lily May, let's get you something to eat, okay? Then you can tell me more. Maybe how they move through time. Or maybe about the man."

"Okay."

"I'll be right back."

"Don't worry, Lily May. He can't hurt you no

more. Me and Della, we made sure of that."

Travis's eyes widened at the sound of the boy's voice. He could hear what sounded like sniffling and small movements in the room before his own voice returned.

"The officer will bring you down to the vending machine. It's not much, but it's convenient and there's a little bit of variety for you to pick from."

Travis hit STOP and waited for Lily May to return from the vending machine. He glanced behind him and stared at the reflective surface of the one-way mirror. No knocks or noises against the glass made him wonder if the man heard what was on the recorder or had he slipped from the room while Lily was gone and missed it. Worse, had he heard it—expected to hear it—and wasn't reacting. Travis considered questioning the man in the other room, but decided against it as Lily appeared in the doorway.

"Thank you for this." She held up a small, prepackaged sandwich in a triangular plastic container and smiled politely but tersely, as she resumed her position in the chair opposite Travis.

Travis nodded and pushed RECORD, hoping Lily didn't see the gooseflesh crawling up his outstretched arm as he wondered what else was on the tape.

"Tell me about Tommy's return." Travis spoke to Lily but looked around the room, wondering if he'd see a shimmering or shadow or any indication of something else in the room with them. He saw nothing and returned his attention to the girl.

Lily pulled back the film at the corner of the container and opened what looked like a ham and cheese sandwich. She pulled the edge up—the cheese, fused to the bread, came with and her efforts tore the softened, mustard-stained dough. She didn't seem to care and plucked bits of lettuce out, dropping them into the plastic container. She methodically picked at the edge of the sandwich, removing the crust all the way around the sandwich and discarding it with the lettuce in the plastic container now serving as her garbage can.

Travis watched in silence, studying her movements and wondering whether they were a nervous action or a normal habit of hers to pick at her food.

Lily shifted her attention to Travis suddenly, as if she'd forgotten he was there waiting for her to talk. "After that first time, Tommy pretty much stayed with me whenever he could. Once he had realized I could see him and talk to him, he said he knew he'd just stay by me. Said he felt safe with me. Like he was scared of something but wouldn't talk about it…or couldn't."

"Some thing or some one?"

Lily looked up at him through the loose strands of hair that had fallen forward as she mangled the sandwich. The dirt from the basement they'd found her in had darkened her hair to a medium brown, but Travis thought it might very well have been a bright blonde when clean.

"I guess someone, not sure why I said something." She shrugged and pulled a small piece of the sandwich free, popping it in her mouth and chewing it with her front teeth, like a mouse nibbling at crumbs. The movement was far too purposeful, and Travis knew she was suddenly pulling back, hiding something. He waited.

She swallowed, pulled another piece off and chewed it while staring at the corner behind him. Travis resisted the urge to follow her gaze—partially from fear, partially to hide his knowledge of the voice on tape.

"Tommy told me he woke up right away, couple days after his funeral I guess, but stayed back and just watched me for a bit before he got too close. Said he was all a wreck and didn't want me seein' him until he could control his looks a bit better. And he done a good job. He don't look dead. He looks just like he did when he was alive. He even had that red shirt on, his favorite—the one I patched the seam on so his

Momma wouldn't get mad we'd tore it playin' in the woods—even though he weren't even buried in it. He looked fine when he finally showed himself to me. And I get it. I know why he waited. But I was mad as a hornet's nest for a time, finding out he'd been there but I didn't know it. And then once I did know, I just wanted to hug him." Her hand went to her throat briefly, her fingertips brushing the locket as they went past, and then she tore off another piece of sandwich. "But I couldn't. I can't. I hate that."

"So he was there near you for a while before you could even see him?"

"Oh yeah, a long time. I guess looking back I kinda knew. Like I could feel him or something. But I couldn't talk to him or see him back then. Couldn't hear or see none of them. That didn't happen until spring."

"Does he know why you could suddenly hear or see the, um, dead? Does he remember what happened to him?"

She put the bite in her mouth and looked down at her lap, shaking her head. "Nah, Tommy didn't know nothin'. Nothin' at all about anythin'."

Lily May slid her chair back, pushing the rest of the sandwich further onto the table, distancing herself from it and Travis.

"Neither of us knew my Papa was gonna pass."

Travis leaned back, trying to appear casual. Friendly. Calm. "Oh?"

She shook her head. "I still don't understand that. I always knew, from the time I was only knee-high, when folk were gonna pass. How could I not know when my own kin was due to die?" She furrowed her brow and met Travis' gaze. "Course, he didn't just up and die, he got real real sick first."

Lily stood and twisted at the waist both directions before stretching her spine as straight and tall as she could. She began to pace, her dirty bare feet making barely a sound on the cold cement floor.

Travis realized he was holding his breath and had frozen all movement, keeping still as if afraid to move and scare the wild animal about to show him its home. He forced his breathing to resume a normal pace and his shoulders to relax.

"There was a lot of commotion one night. Woke me up before the moon had even gotten comfortable in the sky. Papa was throwin' up blood, a lot of blood, and looked real strange. His skin looked like he'd been swimmin' in the old iron pond—you know, that rain-filled gravel pit down by the abandoned mines that makes yer skin all yellow? Mamma dragged him out to the car. She was all cryin' and upset. Meemaw told me to sit tight, that they'd be back, murmuring something about it "taking long enough" on her way out the screen door. Thing was, Mamma and Meemaw came back. Papa didn't."

She paused and leaned against the wall, facing him and the one-way mirror as if waiting for the rest of the line up to join her. "He didn't die that night. He didn't die for almost a week. But he never did leave that hospital room again. I heard people saying he'd done drunk himself to death—burned his liver right out and started bleeding inside. But I don't know. There was something in his eyes those last few weeks. Somethin' just not right.

"And Tommy stayed with me the whole time. When I went to sleep he was sitting against the corner of my room, chin on his pulled up knees. When I woke he was already pacing, waiting for me to join him for the day. He went with me to the hospital the two times I went to see Papa before he died. He went to the funeral with me and cried strange little ghost tears while hoverin' close enough I could almost smell him. And he sat with me at the grave, as I waited almost a week for those flowers to die, for Papa to come back like Tommy had," She sighed. "He didn't."

Travis cocked his head to the side like a confused dog. "Really?"

She just nodded, pulling up one side of her mouth in thought.

"I figured maybe he didn't have no unfinished business or missed good-byes. We stopped going to the graveyard, but Tommy didn't go away, he was always with me. Every single day. Right up to the day I was grabbed right there on Main Street in broad daylight."

"This is when you were kidnapped then?" Travis grabbed the pen and pad, but put them back down when the expression on her face changed at his movement. The recorder would be enough. She was young and scared. He needed her to feel relaxed, just telling a story, not being interrogated.

"This is the part you wanna know about." She looked at him with clear eyes, not blinking as she watched him.

Travis nodded at the statement, acknowledging the question and the reason she'd refused to make it one. She nodded back at him as her face relaxed and her voice softened.

"I didn't see the Shadow Man when he grabbed me. I didn't actually see him for a couple days. It was so fast, so shockin', when that car door opened. It felt like my arm was being yanked off the way he grabbed me right above the elbow and pulled me in. He hit my head on the dash when he did it. I don't know if it was on purpose to knock me out, or a happy accident that made the rest of the trip easier for him. I didn't wake up again until I was tied to that chair in the basement with nothin' but a dripping pipe somewhere in the dark to keep me company."

Lily slid down the wall, folding up behind her legs, arms wrapped around her knees, and lifted her wide-eyed face up toward Travis. The far off look in her expression let him know she wasn't seeing the aesthetically boring gray and white of the interrogation room, but instead was reliving the details of the dirty ten-by-twenty dungeon she'd been kept in.

"He didn't talk to me for two days, ya know. Not a word. He would come down, pull the cord on the hanging light bulb by the stairs, and then walk toward me with the dim light behind him, making him nothing but a cutout. A silhouette. A shadow. He dragged a stool from the corner— the legs scratching their way through the packed dirt on the floor seemed so loud in the quiet. He sat in front of me and pulled the gag from my mouth only to shove a spoon into it. He did it just so, so's I had no time to think or scream, just swallow. And that's how I ate. When I ate. Bland chicken soup with broken flat noodles he probably dumped out of a dented can from the Safe-Way clearance aisle, shoved quickly into my mouth so I didn't have no time to scream."

Lily paused, her mouth slightly open as if to say something, but instead swallowed loud enough for Travis to hear before continuing.

"On the second day. After he fed me the lukewarm soup and wiped my mouth, he asked me what I knew about Tommy's death. He leaned in real close. Too close. I could smell the rot from teeth gone bad. Not bad breath, but bad teeth, like when a dog gets old and pants that hot stink on you. Stink stronger than the smell of my own pee from the bucket he put under the chair for me. He said he didn't want to hurt me, or kill me, but that I had to tell him what I knew about Tommy's murder." Lily's eyes swam into focus, and she looked up at Travis. "He said murder. He knew it was murder."

Travis thinned his lips and said nothing, understanding her adamancy earlier about the distinction between Tommy dying and Tommy being killed.

"I guess I knew right then he was either the man that done killed Tommy, or he knew him. Was protecting him maybe. And I cried. I remember that. I cried because Tommy was dead, even though he had been for months by then, but it seemed to come back and hit me real hard. I cried because this man in the shadows scared me, scared me more than I'd ever remembered being afraid of anything or anyone, including my Papa when he'd been gone drinking for days and come back in the dark of night with an empty bottle and eager fist. I didn't think the Shadow Man was going to let me go. Couldn't believe his words. I couldn't hear his thoughts 'cos the living had gone quiet, and I could only hear the dead. And the dead weren't nowhere to be seen."

"Tommy wasn't there with you when you were grabbed?"

"No, he was. We was walking down the sidewalk together heading back to the house from the graveyard. I don't know what happened to Tommy, but when I woke up tied to that chair, he wasn't there."

Travis nodded.

"The Shadow Man didn't know Tommy was with me. No one knew I could even hear the dead, 'cept for the dead themselves. That news hadn't gotten out, oh Lord's no. But everyone thought I could still hear the living. I suspected the man thought I'd heard something, just like Tommy's mom and everyone else who kept getting mad at me 'cos I shoulda known who did it, but I didn't."

Lily's breathing had sped up with the panic of her speech and emotion in her words as she talked about Tommy's death. She went quiet for a few moments and calmed back down, her gaze occasionally flitting to her hand, which now lay palm up next to her, the fingers curling and uncurling as if holding a hand.

"For the first few days, the man fed me twice a day and asked me the same questions after each feeding. Then he left the light on and didn't come back for a long time. The room was usually in darkness. He was always in shadow—always in the dark edge of the light's little bit of broken glow. But the day he left the light on, as he walked past it, I got a better look at him. Not his face, mind you, but his build, his clothes, his skin.

"I knew he worked a broom or something clean like that 'cos his hands weren't dirty or stained with grease like my Papa's always were after working on the car or messin' with the furnace. That kind of work don't just wash off, ya know. It stains the creases of your skin and stays under the nails even when you scrub 'em. It becomes part of you, part of who ya are. The man didn't have that. He had clean hands. Clean hands and bad breath. Heavy shoulders but not wide, like he'd been muscular at some point maybe. And when he passed that light bulb, I saw the outline of a patch on his back. The shape reminded me of those blue and white squares on the back of the distributor driver's uniforms. I took it all in. Every little thing I could see or smell. I twisted it all around like a puzzle trying to figure out who this was, or if I even knew him."

She sighed.

"I couldn't come up with nothin'. And if I didn't know who it was, then no one would know where to look for me."

Lily brought her hands up to her face and covered the escaping sobs. Travis thought about walking over, bending down, and offering a pat on her shoulder, but worried a man touching her in this state would do more damage than good. He sat where he was. He waited.

She sniffled and stood up, moving back to the chair at the table. She sat without sliding the chair forward and used the napkin to wipe her face.

"I got real scared when I realized that. I screamed inside my head, behind that dirty gag that smelled of chicken soup and dust. I pushed my fear and thoughts out there trying to catch any passing ghosts. I figured if I could hear them, they could hear me. When that didn't seem to work, I tried to push at the living. I mean, if I'd always been able to pull things from people's minds, maybe I could put things there. I tried everything I could think of for a couple days.

"Then the man came and fed me again. I was starving. It had been a couple days. When he was done, he questioned me again, this time slapping me a couple times, either to get his point across or out of frustration, I don't know. And when he left, I went back to screaming inside for help. Must have been about a week when I got tired and stopped yelling for the dead to hear me. I started lookin' at the dirt floor and dirt clinging to everything I could see in that dingy yellow light—from the chair to the walls to the edge of the stairway. I was gone, forgotten, and surrounded by dirt. Basically dead and buried.

"Then I heard Tommy screaming for me."

Lily looked to her left and smiled.

"He came through the doorway at the top of the stairs and raced toward me. I think in that moment he wanted to hug me as much as I'd been itching to hug him. He said when the man took me, he drove away so fast it startled Tommy, and he tried to run after him but lost him. He got all confused and scared, and completely forgot until later that night he could have just been in the car with me if he'd wanted. Rules don't apply to them. They don't have to walk or run, just think it and be there. But by the time he remembered that, he didn't know where I was. He said he started just going through every single house in the direction the car had gone until he finally found me. He told me I was a couple miles outta town on a dirt road he almost didn't even see. He couldn't save me, but at least I wasn't alone no more."

"Couldn't save... oh. I see."

Lily raised an eyebrow at him like he was daft, and continued.

"Tommy said I had been gone for eight days at that point but that my Mamma was looking for me and causing a big stink with the Sheriff. He said Pastor Jacob had the whole church praying for me, and even Miss Betty had come 'round and asked my Mamma if she could do anythin', offerin' a fresh pie from the restaurant as comfort food.

"But they weren't looking in the right place. Not even the right direction, Tommy said. And then he sat right down in the dirt next to me and started telling me stories of all the things he'd done after he died—in the time before I could see him. He kept me company, never leaving my side while I was awake. When I slept, he went to check on my Momma, coming back to tell me she and Meemaw hadn't given up but were no closer. He was almost always there when the man would come down and questioned me, but the man scared him so he'd back up to the dark corner and wait for him to leave. Said the smell of him scared him. I never did tell him who I thought it was, I guess I figured he knew.

"Then the man started yelling at me instead of questionin' me. His slaps started to get harder. And the time he closed his fist, I didn't see the ring on his finger so much as feel it against the side of my face. When I woke up, Tommy was crying next to me. He needed to do something to get me out of there, and he didn't know what. He just knew he didn't trust the man anymore than I did."

Lily looked to her left again, her face painted with an expression a mother would give a hurt child—concern and love.

"The man left me alone for a couple days again, this time leaving the light off. I know Tommy was there, he talked to me and tried to calm me down. But I was gagged and couldn't talk directly, only with thoughts. And it was dark so I couldn't see him. I don't even know how long it was dark like that. No noises upstairs at all. Like the man had left…" She stopped and looked at the sandwich in front of her as if she didn't know what it was or how it had gotten there.

"You were close about the patch on the back of his shirt," Travis offered information to let her take a mental break. "It wasn't a patch from the distributor but from Package Plus, the delivery service that drives to the extreme rural areas. It probably was days, rather than just feeling like it, when you were left alone. His schedule was part-time, on two, off five."

She blinked at his words but he didn't think she absorbed them so much as let them bounce off her, while her mind spun in other directions of memories, pain and fear.

"When he came back he was angry. Real angry. He didn't bring soup. He didn't even remove the gag. He just started swinging. He hit me so hard he knocked the chair over with me tied to it, sending the bucket the other way to spill pee into the dirt floor. He seemed to blame me for that and screamed at me while yanking me back upright. He stomped on my foot and squeezed my wrist, calling it the "vice of truth." All the while asking me what I knew, what I'd heard, about Tommy's murder. When he kicked out at me, hitting my leg and the chair at once, sending me backward onto the floor and breaking the chair, Tommy came from the corner swinging, as if to hit this man back for what he was doing to me.

"Except when Tommy got close enough to finally see him, his eyes widened as much as his mouth and he let out a howl as he scrambled to a stop and backed up, falling over and mimicking me laying on his back in the dirt."

Lily leaned forward and held Travis's gaze tight.

"I ain't never seen a ghost look scared of anything. Or seen one jump out of shock like Tommy did. Hell, I'd never seen the living with as much fear as Tommy had. And as the man stormed back up the stairs, slamming the door at the top, Tommy crawled toward me and the broken chair. He reached for me and started crying the moment his hand went through me, saying 'That's him, Lily May. That's the man what spun my head.'."

"So he hadn't seen the man until then?" Travis queried, but he knew Lily May would keep talking without the polite prodding.

She shook her head. "He'd always been scared o' him and kept clear, hidin' in the back shadows whenever the man came downstairs to feed me—or question me. But now he knew who it was. Now I knew, too. What I only thought might be true, was as real as the fear that crawled outta Tommy's eyes. It was slow at first, like it took him a minute to realize, then the fear shot outta him like the first hatch of pine snakes slithering outta the dead leaves of winter." Lily glanced to her left again with a sad expression of strength. "And now that we both knew who we were dealing with, it was time to do something about it."

She turned her attention back to Travis.

"In truth, Tommy cried for a bit more before we could really react to anythin'. But he's just a little boy. You can't expect no less from him. After he calmed down a bit, he started rememberin' what happened that day.

"He said he didn't know the man. Ain't never seen him before that day at the fair. He was headin' over to the little rusty Ferris wheel—you know, the smaller one they have for kids—where it was set up at the edge by the long sideshow tents. The man grabbed his arm and yanked him into the tall weeds there behind the bearded lady's sign.

"You know she don't really have a beard, right? It's just glued on there. I heard the older kids down at Miss Betty's say the lady was bare, you know…below… 'cos it's all glued above." Lily raised an eyebrow and motioned to her lap with her eyes.

Travis unwittingly mimicked her raised brow expression. He'd always heard the beard was fake, but never that particular theory regarding the source of the hair.

"Anyway, the man grabbed him—holding onto his arm and covering his mouth with his other hand, Tommy said it smelled of pickled eggs and grease—and told him he was gonna take him away from there. Like he was gonna just bring him home an' keep him. Tommy fought the man, and while he was strugglin' against him—I imagine his scrawny little arms and legs were just flailin' like a fish on a hook—he got hit pretty hard in the head. Said he remembered losin' his balance when he got hit and fallin' over and banging on one of those big ol' rail spikes they use to keep the tent ropes to the ground. Tommy said he heard it more than felt it, and he wasn't even sure where exactly it hit him.

"He woke up again about halfway through the field, the man dragging him by one arm real low through the grass. He started twisting and turning and trying to break outta the man's grip, but he had Tommy fast. Tommy reached out and grabbed at the weeds and found an old root stickin' out he could hold and pull against. That just seemed to make the man angry. Tommy said he got that same red-eyed devil look my papa used to get when he'd been drinkin' the better part of the day. The man dropped Tommy's arm and grabbed him by the hair instead. Tommy didn't even remember screaming at that point, but must have been 'cos the man slapped his other hand over Tommy's mouth. And when the man yanked to jerk Tommy off the root, he pulled too hard, too fast—holding Tommy's head the way he was by the hair behind and jaw in front—and Tommy heard a horrible noise behind his ears. I 'spect the man's strength was just too much for Tommy's little neck bones. After that Tommy just remembered being at his grave. And when he finished telling me all that, he started crying all over again."

She stopped, took a deep breath and sighed through barely open lips.

"To hear Tommy tell it, I don't think the man meant to kill him. But he sure didn't feel no guilt about it by the time he grabbed me. And he didn't seem to have no problem hurtin' me to get the answers he was after. Accident or not though, that man was a bad man… Just some bad man. Not even someone important. It wasn't someone we knew. Not his Pa or a teacher, or anyone I recognized from church—which makes me wonder who the heck I heard that day if it weren't him. It was just some random bad man that decided to up and take, and then kill, little Tommy Jenkins that day for no reason other than the wind blew from the east instead o' the west."

Lily May looked to her left again, then slowly around the room, as if watching someone walk behind Travis and then stop by the door.

Travis had to force himself not to follow her gaze to see if he could detect even a ripple of strangeness in the air, but he wanted to so badly he could almost taste the curiosity—an acrid flavor that reminded him of his father's forbidden tool shed. A part of him ached to believe her about Tommy's ghost, wanted to accept what he'd heard with his own ears on the recorder as truth, believed in her innocence. But another part of him wouldn't allow that kind of fantasy or folly to enter his facts-only mindset. He stuck to what could be proven, and focused on what he'd been told, looking straight at the girl and refusing to follow her lead around the room. The most he could do, the only whim he'd allow him, was when he decided to offer up a bit of those facts to Lily May—not sure if he was looking to comfort her or see if she reacted.

"You may not have known him, but you're correct about him being a bad man. His prints were in the system. He was wanted for questioning in two other counties. He might have been nobody to you, but he was definitely somebody."

Lily May looked down and nodded, a slow appreciative nod, as if she were adding a piece to a mental puzzle. She looked back up at Travis, her hand flitting to her locket as she did so.

"When Tommy finally stopped crying the second time, we tried to come up with a plan. The man didn't know Tommy was there, and we thought that had to be helpful in some way. But the man was convinced I could hear his inside voice, and he thought I knew what he'd done. Funny thing was, I couldn't hear the living at all—not since the dead started talking. So the more he questioned, the more he probably thought I was digging around in there.

"Tommy and me knew the man would kill me. We agreed to that almost as soon as we figured out who he was. There weren't no good reason he'd take me, question me like that, and then let me go. He wanted to know what I knew, who I told, and then he'd kill me with no more care than he'd had over Tommy's death, accidental or not. So Tommy left to find someone who could get me out of there. Someone, anyone, who could help us.

"Now bein' as how the only two that could hear other people, dead or alive, were me—tied up and useless—and Tommy, nothin' but a ghost himself, I wasn't sure what exactly Tommy would do. According to Della, when she come to see me, he'd gone back to town and basically rattled every ghost he could find to try and get help. He'd even begged the darker scary ones we usually stayed away from, and stopped at the church steps to ask the older woman but couldn't find her. Then he screamed, hollered, jumped up and down, knocked things over, and slammed the doors of every breathin' soul he thought might understand what was goin' on. None of the livin' caught on. And the dead, so Della said, were just as helpless. The best they could do was move stuff, little stuff. And those that could hop back in time..." Lily May stopped and snapped her attention to the door, eyes widening for a moment.

Her reaction when she'd mentioned the time travel was the same as that moment on the recorder, and Travis couldn't help but look this time. Nothing shimmered or seemed out of place. No haziness or shadowy presence was noticeable. His gaze went from the door, to Lily May, to the recorder on the table, and he hoped it heard what he could not see.

"Anyway, even those who could change things couldn't help this time. Della said there were rules, and something about the dead being too involved—I'm guessing she meant Tommy. Della stayed with me though, cooing and reassurin' me everyone was looking for me, and promising they'd find me soon. I caught her looking around the dark basement and shaking her head, her brow crunched up like she smelled something bad, but I know she can't smell nothing. Did I tell you that? They can't smell or taste, and that's one of the things they complain about the most. All the flavors they miss, or the way their wife or husband smelled that they can't quite grab onto anymore."

Lily May looked at him and unconsciously sniffed the air of the little room. He wasn't sure what she pulled from it, if anything. Travis only noticed the cold cement smell, and the distinct lack of fear, which usually filled the room even when an innocent witness was being questioned.

"Anyways, when Tommy returned a couple days later, Della left, and none too soon. I heard the man come home through the floorboards above me, walking around, slamming things and stomping. He was mad. I didn't know if something happened while he'd been gone—judging' by my grumblin' stomach it had only been a day or two—and I was pretty sure he was gonna take it out on me."

Lily May pushed her back into the chair and hunched slightly, becoming smaller in stature. Travis thought it seemed she was trying to shrink away from the world at large rather than just the conversation.

"You okay?" He leaned forward, putting a

hand on the table but not quite sliding it across for comfort.

"Yeah. I just… the man was so angry. And everything happened so very fast."

Lily picked up the open can of lemon-lime soda she'd gotten with her sandwich and stared into the open hole as if trying to find the answers to life, the universe, and everything else inside. She finally lifted it to her lips, took a long but shallow drink, and put it down with a sigh.

"When the man came down the steps it was with a heavy thud on each plank of wood, I figured it would be the last time I saw him. I figured for sure I was gonna be dead when he went back up them stairs. He sent the light bulb swinging on it's cord when he pushed past it, and was to me in only a few long steps—reaching out and grabbing both my shoulders so quick I didn't even have time to flinch. He held me real hard. Mean like. His thumbs dug into my bones while his fingers squeezed my muscles like those clamps Mamma uses to keep the pickle kettle closed. I'm sure I have bruises, though I still don't feel much of anything but cold. Then the man opened his mouth to speak, but if he did I didn't hear him—I was too busy elsewhere."

Lily May's eyes glassed over, and Travis watched her focus fade off to somewhere else.

"I smelled Papa before I saw him."

"Your papa? But isn't he…" Travis stopped. Lily May looked irritated as her gaze swam back into focus and pierced him with an expression that stopped his question. He couldn't tell if she was upset he'd interrupted an especially difficult part of her story, or believed him stupid for not following along. He motioned her to continue with his hands and kept his questions at bay.

"Like I said, I smelled him first. The stale cigarettes and cheap beer swept through the dark air down there like someone had dumped over the trash can on the back porch. You know Mamma wouldn't let him smoke inside, so he tended to sit out there and light one after another while he drank his way through a case of beer and tried to forget whatever it was that always haunted his eyes.

"But I didn't have no time to find him in the dim light of that dirty basement. No time to say hello or see how he looked. Next I knew I could feel him pushin' his way into my mind, inside my bones, and suddenly I was very far away from everything. Like I was an echo. Or a ghost myself. I was still behind my eyes, still watching from my body, but I wasn't in charge of anything, not my words, not my actions. And I heard my voice on the outside, but my papa's on the inside tell that man a lie that was meant to do nothing but enrage him. Papa told that man that everyone in town knew about him and what he did."

She shook her head but was still talking to her own memories rather than to Travis.

"I can't tell you the last time I ever seen a look on someone that scared me so bad. The man looked like the Devil himself had taken hold, with fire and brimstone in his eyes, and he slammed his big ol' fist across my face before I even realized he'd let go of my shoulders. I went topplin' over backward, chair and all, for the second time. But this time, I slammed into the floor hard enough for the chair to break and my arms to be free of the rope."

Lily May's hand went up to her jaw line and Travis matched her story to the bruise amidst the dirt and grime there.

"My body jumped up from the ground—and I do mean my body, not me, 'cos I weren't in control of nothing—and went straight for that man. I didn't scream and flail like I wanted, like I would have if it had been up to me. No. Instead, I rushed this giant of a man as if he were the same size as me, and we were just tussling on the field after a bad ball game. It seemed like I climbed right up the front of him, knocking him over out of shock, and landed on his chest. From above him, I watched as my hands curled into fists and hit him in the face several times before they went around his neck and squeezed. My Lord did they squeeze. My fingers still hurt a little from the pressure of it. And the whole time, the man is hitting my head and sides and trying to get me off of him, but my hands were locked by my papa's spirit and weren't going no where. And Papa? He weren't being quiet about it, neither—telling the man exactly who he was and how he was gonna kill him first, then torture him once he was a ghost. That he'd punish him until one or the other finally faded to nothing, 'cos neither of them was going to heaven and with no where to go, what better way to spend his time than hurting the man that hurt his little flower."

She blinked, focusing on the present and glanced up at Travis. Her eyes filled with tears but she held her composure and didn't let them fall.

"You have any idea how weird it is to hear someone else in your head with your own voice coming out your mouth?"

Travis just shook his head, suddenly overwhelmed by the memory of the note he'd seen on the paperwork that had made no sense to him at the time. The man had told the first paramedic on the scene, "Ain't no child, that's a she-devil in league with Satan. There ain't no other reason or way no girl that age should ever smell like a dirty ashtray in an old tavern and have strength of a grown man." The medic swore he'd heard those words, but the man lost consciousness before anyone else could ask him to clarify. Travis glanced at the glass behind him and wondered if the man in the shadows back there had read that part of the report and caught Lily's reference to her father's smell.

"So Papa kept yelling at him while he squeezed my hands. The man's eyes got kinda buggy looking, and he started crying—not that kind of crying where you're upset or something, but like when you get pollen in your face or dust from a barn and your eyes just water up all crazy like. It seemed like forever that the man kept kickin' and swingin', but eventually his arms didn't seem to have as much power behind them when they hit me. And then the man stopped struggling, his eyes rollin' back in his head. My hands stayed as they were for a few more seconds before finally letting go. Even in that dim light, I could see red marks on his skin from my hands. My papa's hands.

"I watched myself reach down and pull the man's wallet from his pocket before a strange electric feeling came over me as I felt my papa pull free of me. I was so cold all of a sudden, like a February wind had gotten to my bones. I turned and there was Papa in his funeral suit, hair brushed with a clean part like I'd never seen while he was alive. Papa looked at me with eyes that were no longer scared of me, but I think maybe for me. "Run, baby. Run." He pointed to the wallet in my shaking hands. "Take that to the sheriff." As I turned to do as I was told, I saw him pull Tommy into his arms and hug him like he was his own flesh and blood.

"I ran so fast, so far. I ran down that dirt road and turned left. I don't even know why I turned left, I just did, and ran and ran and ran, until a car stopped and a woman told me to get in.

"I don't even know who it was. Who brought me here?

"And I didn't even tell her to bring me home. Or to the hospital. I told her to bring me here, like my papa said. I went straight to the sheriff and gave them that wallet. I heard they went out and got the man. That an ambulance brought him back to the hospital…"

Lily May looked up at Travis, her eyes full of something he could only call hope, but he didn't know what they hoped for. Did she wish he was still alive? Was she worried about killing him? Did she know?

"They did go out." Travis offered. "Two squads, because they thought they were just going to pick up a kidnapper. They called for an ambulance when they found him in the living room bleeding out."

"Bleeding? He weren't bleeding when I ran out of there. He weren't upstairs, neither. I left him down in the dirt."

"He was bleeding pretty bad. There was a

tire iron in his hand and matching marks on his shoulder and forehead. He spoke briefly, said a couple of crazy things but enough coherent things to confirm he did indeed kill Tommy Jenkins. He died in the ambulance on the way back to the hospital."

"He died?"

Travis nodded and watched her, looking for glee or relief but seeing nothing but sadness and remorse. And confusion.

"But I left him downstairs…"

Travis stood, keeping his eyes on her. If she'd left him in the basement and he'd crawled to the living room, then who had beat him? The tire iron was in his own hand. The initial report from the officers on scene said it was suspected the tire iron was either for self-defense or as a weapon of intent against Lily. But if she claimed to have left him in the basement and only strangled him, without any mention of a weapon other than her hands. Oh, but if Lily's papa… If he really did possess Lily, could he have… Nah.

"You sure you don't want a lawyer or a public defendant or anything? I mean, I know you think you didn't do anything, but a man is dead. And you've confessed to choking him. If the autopsy shows strangulation led to or was involved with his death…"

"I didn't do nothin' wrong! Momma says

she's getting someone to help if it comes to that, but I didn't do nothin'. He was unconscious, but breathing, when I left him. Is Momma still here?"

Lily May's reaction was fierce, full of emotion but equally saturated with a desperate plea for him to believe her words. All of them. He softened his voice. "Yes, she's out in the waiting area. I'll be right back." Travis gathered the trash from the sandwich she'd only barely eaten. "Do you want another soda or water?"

Lily May shook her head and fiddled with her locket. Her eyes seemed glued to the corner of the table.

Travis dropped the trash in the lined can outside the door and immediately opened the adjoining room. He looked both ways in the hall and stepped inside, not bothering to shut the door behind him.

"So?" Travis questioned the man he couldn't see. "Do we believe her? 'Cos as convincing as she is, I ain't been to church in a long while and I'm having a hell of a time believing she could talk to ghosts, let alone be possessed by one."

"Let me ask you, Detective Butler, did you at any time question whether you believed her? Did her story or any of the details hit you just right and make you question your own beliefs?" The ornamental steel at the tip of the cowboy boot poking out of the darkness began to move fluidly, as if the man were swinging a leg casually but it came off more condescending than relaxed.

Travis said nothing. He had indeed questioned things. He had to remind himself a couple times to stick to the facts.

"See? You're not answering. Which means you did hesitate. And if you—a cop trained to follow only the facts—wavered, what do you suppose a jury will do? And to a child no less. A child who was abducted and abused for two weeks. She'll walk."

"My god, she could say anything she wanted…" Travis felt the system he believed in crumble in his mind.

"Yes. And that would be a horrible travesty. Unless she's telling us the truth."

Travis cocked his head at the figure in the shadows. "Truth?"

"What if she can talk to the dead? Or hear the living? Just think…" The man paused and Travis felt the question hang before him in the darkness. "But right now it's just a fluctuation of confidence, a question of beliefs. It's not proof. Go back. Go keep her company. Tell her we're bringing in a doctor to look her over. See what kind of small talk you can get her to indulge in."

Travis nodded, wondering again if the man in the shadows had heard what was on the playback. The voice that recorded. The voice that may or may not be considered proof. Travis didn't ask, didn't offer the information, and simply slipped back out into the hallway, closing the door without a sound before returning to the interrogation room.

"Lily May, is there anything else you'd like to tell me about while we wait? Seems they're going to bring in a couple other people to talk to you."

Travis sat back down, pushing the notebook away as unnecessary at this point, and pondered the situation. She's old enough to be tried as an adult, and there would be a trial even with the abduction because of the circumstances surrounding the death of her kidnapper—if for no other reason than her story not quite matching the crime scene. The damn tire iron threw everything off. And the ghosts. She could very easily say self-defense, starvation, desperation, any number of things as an excuse for both killing him and leaving out details of how, leaving out the tire iron, or lying about where he was when she left. But the second she mentions ghosts in a court of law they're going to assume she's…nuts.

"I'm not nuts."

Travis snapped his attention to her and noticed her furrowed brow and folded hands. Like an angry calm had washed over her.

"And anyone that claims insanity as an

excuse to kill someone is still guilty of murder. Still going to hell."

"But…" Travis leaned forward, his expression tightening with concern and wonder as he lowered his voice to a whisper, forgetting the recorder was between them and catching everything anyway. "I didn't say that out loud."

"No, you didn't. But you didn't let me finish telling you my story." Lily May sat up and looked over his shoulder at the mirror while she spoke, not whispering at all, but speaking clearer than she had through the entire interview. "When Papa left me, when he pulled free with a sting that felt like that time I stuck a darning needle in the wall socket to see what would happen and shocked myself silly, well, he took whatever walls I had with him. I can hear the living and the dead just fine now. It's been a bit tricky since I got back to town this mornin'. I'm always lookin' around tryin' to figure out if what I'm hearing is alive or not, but I'm starting to figure out the difference in the way it tickles my ears."

Travis sat back, worry washing across his face like a breeze sending ripples across a calm pond. He was the proof they were looking for. They'd brought him in on this case for a reason and now he understood that reason.

"And you should worry. You may be from out of the county and therefore supposed to be objective, but you have your own little dark secrets, don't you?" Lily May hunched over the table and returned his whisper. "But Charlotte forgave you, ya know. And you'd get over it a whole lot faster if you forgave yourself."

He sat bolt upright, his eyes widening in disbelief. "How? How do you know about Charlotte?"

"You think really loud." Lily May smiled. "It was just an accident. She knows that. And she knows you loved her, still love her. But there's other things you think about that are smudged in gray and sin. Things the man behind that glass would use against you. Things that would change your future, your life, if anyone other than me ever heard them."

Travis squinted an eye at her. He knew it was impossible to not think of Charlotte, especially when looking at Lily May who reminded him of everything innocent and whimsical about the women he'd loved and lost. But he hadn't been thinking of his other sins. Or at least he hadn't thought so. Trying to not think of them was more difficult than he'd imagined, but he attempted to keep the imagery in his mind muddy as he wondered which of the black marks on his soul she had picked up.

"Do you want me to tell you which ones?" She grinned.

He knew it was the innocent smile of a child trying to be helpful, but it felt almost wicked, self-serving. He opened his mouth to speak but the door opened and startled him.

Two men in dark suits walked in and stepped to either side of the door, allowing a third to come between them and fully enter the room. The two to the sides could have been twins— boring interchangeable twins with dark hair cut in the same nondescript fashion and suits purchased off the rack for mandatory wear on the job.

The third man's suit was anything but boring. He wore black pants and jacket with an expensive looking cream-colored shirt underneath, no tie, and all of it fitted by a talented tailor. His hair was almost the same color as his shirt and Travis recognized it as what his mother would have called "bottled gray-be-gone"—not really blonde, but meant to be, meant to hide the silver and gray that had taken over whatever color had originally been there. The shiny cowboy boots poking out of the bottom of his pleated slacks let Travis know this was the man who had been listening from the shadows. He looked directly at Travis, ignoring the girl whose wide eyes studied him.

"Self-defense. Innocent. No need for a trial. Write it up."

He turned and smiled at Lily May, holding his hand out for her to take. "If you could come with us, little lady."

Much to Travis' surprise, Lily May reached across the table and grabbed his hand as she reached for the tall man's outstretched fingers. Travis' vision blurred, and Lily May's face was replaced with the fuzzy image of a long hallway, a large wooden desk with a smiling woman behind it, and several children running from room to room with books in their hands. The image scrambled and was replaced with a clean white room filled with smiling doctors and content children—the doctors writing on clipboards, the children sitting with legs swinging. The scenery moved again, to what Travis could only assume was the exterior. He saw a large stone building, which stretched out against perfectly green grass before turning into an L-wing at the right end. The center of the building jutted up to a clock tower in the clouds, with a large copper plaque under the clock which read: McMillan Hall. His vision shimmied and Lily May was smiling at him before he realized she'd let go of his hand.

He'd believed the man in the shadows was a cop, or perhaps a lawyer, but what Lily had showed him, with the added details of the twin suits to his side, made Travis change his opinion. This man was government. And that, Travis thought, was much more dangerous to Lily May than the D.A. could ever have been.

Lily May looked up at the man from the

shadows, "I don't know if it's really all true, but you certainly believe it is…" She nodded and stood, looking behind her at the corner. "Can Tommy come, too?"

Lily May leaned across the table and whispered, not taking her eyes from the corner. "You'll visit?"

Travis nodded and looked at the corner where her eyes were locked. There sat a small, thin boy in a tattered red shirt, his hair tousled, his expression a beam of love in Lily May's direction. Tommy. Why? Why can I see him? Did she allow me to tap into her sight by touching me? Before he could ask Lily May with anything more than a puzzled look, Tommy stood up and fell in line behind the girl who loved him in life and death.

The man from the shadows spoke with authority, the men beside him giving each other sideways glances that let Travis know they weren't privy to anything that had been said, recorded, or observed. "Absolutely dear. We wouldn't dream of leaving him behind."

Lily turned slowly to Travis before pulling her hand from his and placing a finger in front of her lips. She smiled behind the gesture and let him know she'd keep his secrets.

Travis slid his chair out to stand, but the twin suits moved forward and the man in the cowboy boots held his other hand up to silently motion, or rather, demand Travis to stay where he was. Travis pivoted toward the girl whose hand seemed to disappear in the grip of the man in front of her.

"Lily May, what did Tommy mean when he said he and Della made it so the man can't hurt you no more?" Letting her know he heard things on the tape and asking a final question before being pushed out of the investigation and into history.

"Easy." She grinned, then turned from Travis to Tommy. "They killed his ghost."

ABOUT THE AUTHOR

Born and raised in Wisconsin, Kelli Owen now lives in Pennsylvania. She's attended countless writing conventions, participated on dozens of panels, and spoken at the CIA Headquarters in Langley, VA. Visit her website at kelliowen.com for more information. F/F

Lily May's story continues in PASSAGES.
Available everywhere, summer 2019.

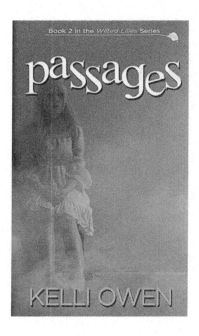

Lily May Holloway can hear the thoughts of
the living, and speak to the dead. She's done so
since she was little, and been shunned for it.

As a new student at McMillan Hall, a private
school with other teens who have a
variety of psychic gifts, she finds she isn't
necessarily unique. Or safe.

Acceptance is no longer her only concern.
Staying alive is.

Made in the USA
Columbia, SC
24 March 2020

89903494R00055